Dear Parents,

Welcome to the Scholastic Reader series. We have taken over 80 years of experience with teachers, parents, and children and put it into a program that is designed to match your child's interests and skills.

Level 1— Short sentences and stories made up of words kids can sound out using their phonics skills and words that are important to remember.

Level 2— Longer sentences and stories with words kids need to know and new "big" words that they will want to know.

Level 3— From sentences to paragraphs to longer stories, these books have large "chunks" of texts and are made up of a rich vocabulary.

Level 4— First chapter books with more words and fewer pictures.

It is important that children learn to read well enough to succeed in school and beyond. Here are ideas for reading this book with your child:

• Look at the book together. Encourage your child to read the title and make a prediction about the story.
• Read the book together. Encourage your child to sound out words when appropriate. When your child struggles, you can help by providing the word.
• Encourage your child to retell the story. This is a great way to check for comprehension.
• Have your child take the fluency test on the last page to check progress.

Scholastic Readers are designed to support your child's efforts to learn how to read at every age and every stage. Enjoy helping your child learn to read and love to read.

— **Francie Alexander**
  Chief Education Officer
  Scholastic Education

For Fluffy's favorite gardener, Shirley Glaser
— K.M.

For Kate, who makes it look easy
— M.S.

Text copyright © 2001 by Kate McMullan.
Illustrations copyright © 2001 by Mavis Smith.
Activities copyright © 2003 Scholastic Inc.
All rights reserved. Published by Scholastic Inc.
SCHOLASTIC, CARTWHEEL BOOKS, FLUFFY THE CLASSROOM GUINEA PIG,
and associated logos are trademarks and/or registered trademarks of Scholastic Inc.

Library of Congress Cataloging-in-Publication Data is available.

ISBN: 0-439-20674-X

10 9 8 7 6 5 4 3   04 05 06 07
Printed in the U.S.A. 23 • First printing, April 2001

FLUFFY
GROWS A GARDEN

by **Kate McMullan**
Illustrated by **Mavis Smith**

Scholastic Reader — Level 3

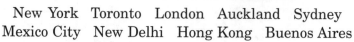

SCHOLASTIC INC. **Cartwheel B·O·O·K·S®**

New York Toronto London Auckland Sydney
Mexico City New Delhi Hong Kong Buenos Aires

I Love Carrots!

"Spring is here," said Ms. Day.

"What happens in the spring?"

"Spring vacation!" said Emma.

"Baseball spring training!" said Wade.

"Plants start to grow," said Maxwell.

"Yes," said Ms. Day.

"This spring we will plant a garden."

Plant carrots! thought Fluffy.

I love carrots!

Everyone in the class
filled paper cups with soil.
They planted seeds in the cups.
They watered the seeds.

"Ms. Day?" said Emma and Jasmine.

"May we plant a garden for Fluffy?"

"Good idea," said Ms. Day.

Great idea! thought Fluffy.

Plant a carrot garden!

The girls took three cups
over to Fluffy's cage.
"What kinds of seeds shall we plant?"
said Emma.
Take a wild guess, thought Fluffy.

"How about marigolds?" said Emma.

Wrong! thought Fluffy.

I can't eat flowers!

Emma and Jasmine planted
marigold seeds.

"Do you like peas, Fluffy?" asked Emma.

Not as much as carrots,

thought Fluffy.

The girls planted pea seeds.

"Now what?" said Jasmine.

Read my lips, thought Fluffy.

CARROT SEEDS!

"Petunias?" said Emma.

No! No! No! thought Fluffy.

He raced over to his food bowl.

He picked up what was left
of a carrot top.

He ran with it over to the girls.

"Yuck," said Jasmine.

"Fluffy brought us his old carrot."

"Hey, I know," said Emma.

"Let's plant carrot seeds for Fluffy."

Bingo! thought Fluffy.

The girls planted carrot seeds.

Emma watered the seeds.
She put the seed cups
into Fluffy's cage.
Grow, carrots! thought Fluffy.

For a while, nothing grew.
Then, one day, green shoots
peeked out of the soil.
They grew bigger and bigger.
Leaves appeared.

These plants are green,
thought Fluffy.
Carrots are orange.
Who stole my carrots?

One sunny day,
Emma carried Fluffy's plants outside.
Jasmine carried Fluffy.
She put him down in the class garden.

Emma dug three holes.
She slid Fluffy's plants out of the cups
and planted them in the holes.
Jasmine watered Fluffy's plants.
Don't water me! thought Fluffy.
I'm not a plant!

Emma wrote the names of the plants
on craft sticks.
She poked the sticks into the soil.
"This is your marigold," she told Fluffy.
"And this is your pea plant."
Big deal, thought Fluffy.

"This is your carrot plant," said Emma.

That? thought Fluffy. **I don't think so.**

"You know carrots grow underground,
right, Fluffy?" said Jasmine.

Underground? thought Fluffy.
**U h . . . I knew that . . .
because I love carrots!**

The Guard of the Garden

On sunny days,
the girls put Fluffy in the garden.
He liked to watch his plants
grow and change.
The marigold grew buds and flowers.
So did the pea plant.
The carrot plant got very bushy.

One day two bees
flew into the garden.
I am the guard of the garden!
Fluffy told the bees. **Buzz off!**
Hold it, pal, said the big bee.
Your garden needs us.

I land on a flower, see?
said the big bee.
While I drink nectar,
my legs get covered in pollen.
Then I visit another flower.
The pollen from the first flower
brushes off my legs
and onto the second flower.
Now the second flower can make
new seeds.

No bees, no seeds,
said the little bee.
Okay, bees, said Fluffy.
Come into my garden.

Fluffy saw two ladybugs.

I am the guard of the garden!

Fly away home! he told the ladybugs.

Not so fast, pig, said the big ladybug.

Your garden needs us.

See those little white bugs on

your pea plant?

Fluffy ran over to his pea plant.
He gasped!
The leaves were covered
with little white bugs.

Those bugs will suck the food out of the leaves, said the big ladybug.

Unless we eat the bugs first, said the little ladybug.

Hurry, ladybugs! said Fluffy.

Save my pea plant!

Fluffy saw a pair of worms.

I am the guard of the garden!
Fluffy told the worms. **Be gone!**

Peace, dude, said the big worm.
Your garden needs us.

We crawl around under the ground,
said the big worm.
We mix air into the soil.
The air makes space for water
to trickle down into the ground.

Down like where carrots grow, dude,
said the little worm.
Carrots? said Fluffy.
Welcome to my garden, worms!

Fluffy lay down
in the shade of his pea plant.
Fluffy watched the bees fly.
He watched the ladybugs eat.
He watched the worms crawl.
Gardening is hard work,
thought Fluffy.
But somebody's got to do it.

PEPPERS

Nice Work, Fluffy!

The days grew warm.
The marigold plant
was covered with flowers.
The pea flowers
had turned into pea pods.
The leaves of the carrot plant were
bigger than ever.
My garden is just right,
thought Fluffy.

Then Fluffy saw two slugs.

They were chewing on his pea plant.

He ran over to them.

I am the guard of the garden!

Fluffy told the slugs.

How does my garden need you?

Burp, said the big slug.

BURP, said the little slug.

The slugs kept chewing.

Scram, slugs! said Fluffy.

And I mean NOW!

He ran at the slugs.

The slimy slugs crawled away.

Emma picked Fluffy up.

"Nice work, Fluffy," she said.

Just doing my job, thought Fluffy.

"Now it is time to harvest the garden,"
Emma said.

Do what? thought Fluffy.

Emma began picking marigolds.

Stop! thought Fluffy.

Jasmine began picking pea pods.

Help! thought Fluffy.

Somebody call the police!

Then Emma reached down.

She took hold of the carrot plant.

What do you think you're doing?

thought Fluffy.

He ran at Emma.

But he was too late.

POP!

Emma pulled up a great big carrot.

Wow! thought Fluffy. **My carrot!**

Ms. Day's class had a feast.
They had a salad with lettuce and
tomatoes.
They had stuffed peppers.
They had mint iced tea.
Almost everything they ate
came from their garden.

Emma and Jasmine
set a place for Fluffy, too.
He had a little pot of marigolds.
He had seven peas.
And he had his great big carrot.
"Dig in, Fluffy," said Emma.

Yum! thought Fluffy.
He could hardly wait to grow
another carrot next spring.